To all the wonderful horses and ponies at Tågra, Alekärr, and Gunnebo Riding Club

Rabén & Sjögren Bokförlag
www.raben.se
Translation copyright © 2001 by Rabén & Sjögren
All rights reserved

Originally published in Sweden by Rabén & Sjögren Bokförlag under the title *Det går framåt, Pontus!*

Text copyright © 1997 by Ann-Sofie Jeppson
Illustrations copyright © 1997 by Catarina Kruusval
Library of Congress card number 2001130143
Printed in Italy
First American edition, 2001
ISBN 91-29-65393-2

ANN-SOFIE JEPPSON • Illustrated by CATARINA KRUUSVAL
Translated by Frances Corry

You're Growing Up, Pontus!

The horse's or pony's "room"—with a door—so it can move around freely

One of the bedding materials you can put on the floor of the stall

BOX STALL

5 box stalls for rent in small, pleasant stable. Free supply of shavings. Hay from own meadows. Arena. Good bridle paths and pastures.
G. Hansson, Lotta Farm,
tel. 164 19.

The most important food for the horse or pony

Outdoor riding school

R&S
BOOKS

Stockholm New York London Adelaide Toronto

HORSE · New Forest · **PONIES** · Russ · Welsh Mountain · Shetland

200 cm
100 cm
0 cm

NEW FOREST • Large English mixed-breed pony. Still living wild in southern England's New Forest. Good riding pony with nice temperament.

WELSH MOUNTAIN • Small Welsh pony. Pretty, fast, and hardy as a riding and driving pony.

SHETLAND • The world's strongest horse for its size. Used for transport in British coal mines during the nineteenth century. Excellent riding and driving pony.

RUSS • Swedish breed originating from the wild ponies living on Gotland. Small, calm, and stubborn.

WATER • SHADE • WIND PROTECTION
Three essentials for horses in pastures. A horse will drink 7 to 13 gallons of water per day.

HAYLAGE • Grass and green plants turned into hay with the help of healthy bacteria and stored for the winter. Kept in either silos—tall towers—or large bales covered with plastic.

SALT LICK • To convert grass into muscles, the horse needs salt. The salt lick is a large brick of salt that horses can lick when they need more salt.

AUGUST 2

I have been out in one of the big pastures all summer long. But soon I won't be allowed to graze anymore. I live with the girl with the yellow mane, and I think she wants to ride me. I just don't know how it is done.

My brother—who is in the pasture next door—has told me what it is like to have a rider on your back. A rider who squeezes her legs to tell you how fast to go. I'll never be able to do that. I'll make mistakes and, besides, I'm ticklish.

Big horses are grazing next to us. Sometimes they come up to the fence and glare at us ponies. We nod at each other when we gallop off. But I've noticed that they also jump and frolic sometimes. Playing is such fun . . .

Yesterday a human dad came running along the fence. We ran after, all of us—faster and faster. Then he turned off toward the forest. But we continued round and round, for a long time. Then we drank nearly all the water in the bucket and each had a lick at the salt lick.

It has been really quiet and peaceful here. The grass and the trees smell wonderful. The large, rumbling machines that rolled over the fields and collected the hay didn't smell nice, though. But the hay will probably taste good next winter.

I would prefer to stay here in the pasture with my new friends. I can remember feeling lonely sometimes in the stable . . .

AUGUST
20

Today the girl with the yellow mane brought me home to the stable. It was both sad and fun. The girl told me I would meet some of my new friends from the pasture on weekends, and one of them would even be moving into my stable. While I walked homeward, I tried to remember what my stable friend, the kitten, looked like: small, soft, and patchy.

The stable didn't look the same, nor did the box stall. I rushed in as usual, but something wasn't right. I backed out again, straight onto the girl's little brother. He was suddenly there behind me. Much too close! Luckily, I didn't trample on him, but he got scared and upset anyway. There was quite a circus in the stable aisle before we dared to rub noses again.

When it got peaceful and quiet, I saw some pellets in the manger. While I chewed and enjoyed them, I looked around. The color of the walls had changed. Everything looked lighter.

Just then, something soft landed in my mane. The kitten! Much bigger, but just as soft as last spring. He lay down on my back and mewed.

His siblings had moved away—two to the farm next door, and one to the girl's little cousin. And now he had a name: Patch. It suits him perfectly.

"Five ponies will be moving in here soon. One is a skewbald, just like me," he mewed, and slunk in under his old broken plank in the wall.

How exciting!

DAPPLE-GRAY • Light gray with black, brown, or red spots or patches in its coat. Horses other than gray can have dapples as well. They are presumed to be a sign of good health.

DUN • Light brown, beige, or yellow coat. All dun and buckskin horses have a dark line along their spine—a so-called eel stripe.

Horses and ponies come in several colors—single colors or patches. The colors have different names. The markings on the legs also have special names.

10

SKEWBALD and PIEBALD • Brown (skewbald) or black (piebald) coat with large irregular white patches.

White fetlock

BLACK • Entirely black coat without any brown or light hairs.

White stocking

BAY • Brown coat and black mane, forelock, and tail.

White coronet

White sock

APPALOOSA • Round, colored spots in a light gray or white coat.

11

Star   Blaze   Snip   White face

Soon the first ponies arrived! A tiny pinto, and then Lisa, who had been in my pasture all summer. Suddenly the whole stable felt different. It was never quiet. It wasn't just the new ponies. There were lots of humans, too, who rattled all the doors. It was quiet only at night. But it would get even worse.

This morning two new ponies arrived: one who was even fatter than I—with a stylish dark line along his back—and another one called Raisin. Raisin brought with him a very small human. She tried to pull Patch's tail. He fled into my stall and jumped up on my back, lost his balance, and stuck all his claws into me to try to hang on. That was painful, I can tell you! So I kicked the wall. The little human was scared and screamed loudly until the little brother came rushing in and carried her outside.

At last there was silence again, and we were fed. All of us stood in our stalls munching and crunching in time. A sleepy-making sound . . .

I woke up when the door next to mine clicked. Outside was a pony of about my size. She looked a bit like me, too, but with a different marking on her forehead. She was called Princess. She came from my old stable and brought greetings from my mom. Mom had just had another foal.

Princess and I whinnied together all evening. This might turn out to be a really good winter!

LUNGING • A way of teaching young horses the different paces and of getting injured horses to start moving again under controlled circumstances. You attach a lunge line to the horse and let him run in circles around you, while you give commands such as "trot" and "canter."

BEAKING IN • The process of training a horse to obey commands so that the horse can be ridden.

OCTOBER
2

Today a new girl came. She is going to break me in. She seems very strict! "Let's start the training now," she said and brought me out to the arena. It was cold, and the ground was frosty. She had lots of clothes on and great big boots. I had nothing on. I could feel my coat prickling from the cold, and I became quite frisky in the clear morning air. She didn't get frisky. She just got even stricter.

This made playing no fun. But just as she was about to attach the lunge line to me, I snuck off . . .

The girl with the yellow mane had to chase me all around the arena. My trainer probably couldn't move inside all those clothes. The girl with the yellow mane got out a handful of pellets from her pocket. That made me come to her! "You mustn't spoil him. Then he'll learn that it pays to be naughty," the trainer said. Why is she always so strict?

VAULTING • Gymnastics at full speed done on horseback. For some movements, the rider holds on to what's called a vaulting roller. One person holds the horse on a lunge line, just as for lunging.

After an hour, my head was spinning, although I had run on both a left-hand rein and a right-hand rein.

Just as we came back into the stable passage, a whole flock of little girls in helmets came running toward us. "Have you been practicing vaulting? Could we come, too? Pleeease!"

The girl with the yellow mane told them that I was only being broken in. Only! And she said that I could not manage yet with children standing on my back. The very idea! As though it wasn't enough with the kitten. I was completely exhausted, and closed my eyes for a bit.

After dinner, Princess asked how it had gone. She is already broken in and gave me some good tips . . .

16

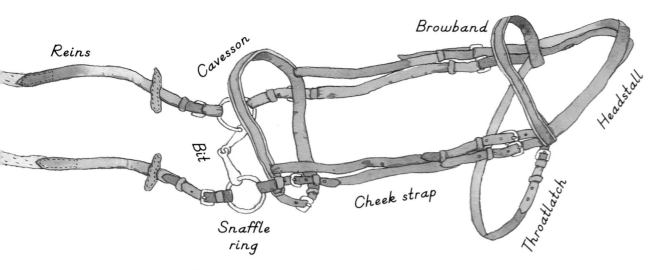

Reins

Cavesson

Browband

Headstall

Bit

Throatlatch

Cheek strap

Snaffle ring

OCTOBER 23

I'm really proud of myself when I think of how much I've learned. Soon I'll be able to enter a show-jumping competition and win—just like my brother.

My trainer is also satisfied: "He's finding it easy to learn, but he's still as frisky as a calf."

Just as I stood thinking about this, sucking on an old, soft piece of carrot, the stall door rattled. A little girl with a brown mane came in with a bridle—a big bundle of leather straps and steel pieces.

She undid my halter and hung it around my neck. Then she dropped the bridle in the shavings. It got all dirty. She picked it up again. I didn't know what was going on.

Then the awful thing happened. She tried to push the big, cold, dirty bit into my mouth—right against my teeth—while hanging on to one of my ears. I panicked. I thought my last moment had come. Suddenly another little girl came into the stall and pulled it all off again and told her not to put a cold, dirty bit in.

After a while she came back with a clean, warm one—and tried pushing it into my mouth again! Then the mom came. She had heard the noise and felt sure that it was me . . .

The girls had gone into the wrong stall! They had been given permission to prepare Princess for a ride. The mom helped them put a saddle and the untangled leather bridle on Princess. I wonder if I'll ever dare let anyone other than the girl with the yellow mane put a bridle on me?

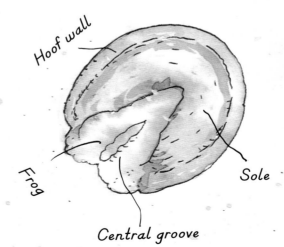

Yesterday the little brother brought a few school friends home. I heard them playing in the yard. After a while the boy came in to me, grabbed hold of my halter, and pulled me out through the door. "They want to see you," he said.

It smelled lovely outside after the rain, and there were wonderful, muddy puddles everywhere in the yard. I felt such an urge to roll . . .

The boy lost his grip, and his friends shouted and laughed as I wallowed in the puddles and gravel.

The dad shouted, too. But he didn't laugh. He took hold of my halter, just as I stood up again, and led me back into my stall.

Later, the little brother came in. Alone, with a bucket of tepid water, brushes, cloths, and a stool. He washed off all the dirt, brushed my featherings, and cleaned underneath my hooves.

It felt good to be pampered. Luckily, he didn't brush under my stomach—I'm so ticklish there. I dozed and listened to him singing and chatting. Finally, he cleared out all the wet shavings and came back with some new.

I think we're becoming really good friends.

When dusk fell, the whole family gathered around my box to admire his work. That evening, Patch fell asleep on my clean back.

*THE HOOF •
Looks like
this underneath:*

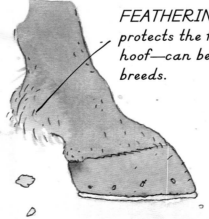

FEATHERING • The hair that protects the fetlock above the hoof—can be very long in some breeds.

HOOF-PICK • Used to clean out the hoof. The brush is used to brush off loose dust.

Hoof wall

Frog

Sole

Central groove

BLANKET • *Keeps the horse warm in the paddock or during transport on cold days.*

COOLER • *Absorbs sweat so that the horse does not freeze after hard riding or driving.*

TURNOUT BLANKET • *The horse's raincoat!*

I'm sick. Very sick. I can feel it all through my body. I was standing in the pasture as usual. It was nice, but a bit cold. The wind increased suddenly, and dark clouds gathered in the sky. Large, wet snowflakes collected on my mane and my tail. Soon sharp hailstones were rattling through the air as well.

I couldn't find cover anywhere. I moved around so my rear end was toward the wind, but it didn't help much. After a while the snow came down heavily and formed soft mounds on fences and posts. Probably on me, too . . . And no one came, however much I neighed!

Later, when it was pitch-black outside, I saw some headlights in the yard at last.

The girl with the yellow mane came running toward me with tears in her eyes. We fought our way to the stable against the wind. I hardly noticed as she rubbed me dry and put one blanket after another on top of me. I could hear her, as though from far away, talking about the car having broken down.

In the night, I got thirsty. When I got up, I saw that someone else was asleep in the stall: the girl with the yellow mane, wrapped up in a horse blanket. I bent over and breathed in her hair. She looked so small and cold, and I was feeling so warm.

DECEMBER 3

The vet has been here! He pushed and prodded me everywhere. Stared hard into my eyes. Took my temperature, looked down my throat, and poured strong medicine into me.

I feel like an empty hay sack. There's no friskiness left in my body. The vet said it is only a bad cold.

22

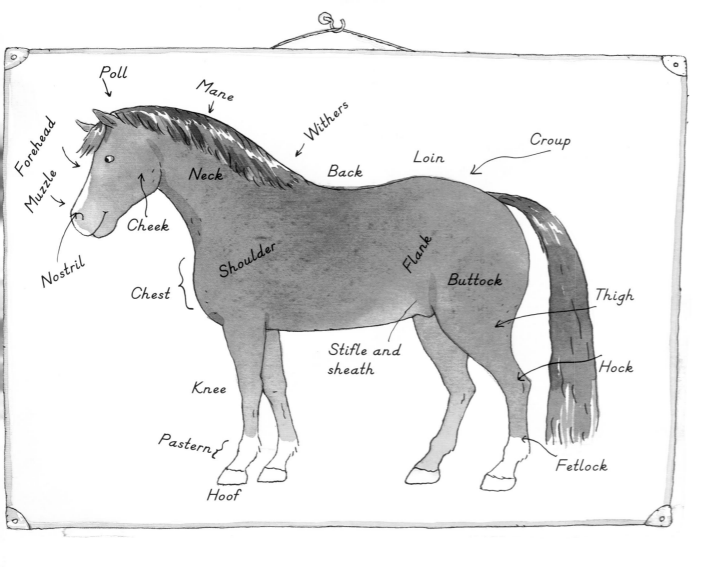

Poll
Mane
Withers
Forehead
Muzzle
Neck
Back
Loin
Croup
Cheek
Nostril
Shoulder
Flank
Buttock
Thigh
Chest
Stifle and sheath
Hock
Knee
Fetlock
Pastern
Hoof

Patch is happy. He thinks that I am so wonderfully warm and calm. He has spent several days in my stall. Outside, it's stormy. In here, all the ponies are unsettled by the whistling wind and by not being allowed out. I'm not worried. But I miss the girl with the yellow mane. She hasn't been here to take of me since she slept in my stall. Her mom has taken care of me, and she told me that the girl has got a cold just as bad as mine.

The little boy came in with a handful of pellets. Yuck—they looked like little sawdust sausages. "You must be really sick," he said, sighing.

The girl with the yellow mane snuffled in toward evening. She hugged me and promised that I would never be left out in the cold again.

"Please forgive me, Pontus," she said. I pushed my nose under her arm, and we stayed like that until I fell asleep.

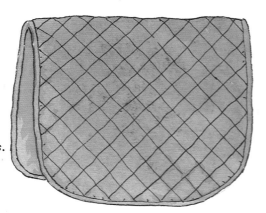

SADDLE BLANKET
Larger type of pad, used for competitions.

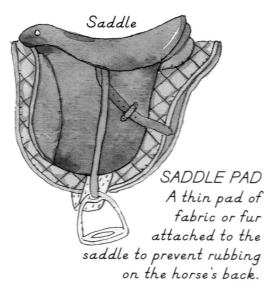

Saddle

SADDLE PAD
A thin pad of fabric or fur attached to the saddle to prevent rubbing on the horse's back.

DECEMBER
24

I'm well again. I can feel it in my legs. They're frisky again. They want to run. I just have to kick the wall. I'm happy. I want to go out again. I've looked out the windows. The snow is deep. There are just some narrow paths cleared across the yard. Outside my window, there's a sheaf of oats. Little birds are jumping and singing in it all day. Red, yellow, and blue little birds. It's a very pretty view.

The inside of the stable is also very nice. And it smells good. The girls spent one whole day putting up decorations for us. They brought shiny red and gold paper, a little fir tree, holly, and evergreens, which they made into garlands. Over all the doors they hung carrots, apples, and bread cakes—much too high up!

Somebody's arriving!

Three little humans in red hats and a little black cat on a leash: the girl with the yellow mane, her little brother, her cousin, and Patch's sister. They have a package with them.

Patch gets a furry mouse, and I get a new red halter and a checked red saddle blanket with "Pontus" written on it. "I made it at school," says the girl. She fetches the saddle. She changes the saddle blanket and looks pleadingly at me from under the hat. Today I nod and allow her to put on the saddle. Imagine me, looking so elegant!

Suddenly the little humans disappear to watch television—whatever that might be.

Patch has already chewed off the mouse's tail and is burying it in the shavings. I lie down beside him.

I wonder if I can reach the bread cakes if I stand on my hind legs. Perhaps I should try tomorrow . . .

It's happened again. There's a piece in the paper about my brother. He won first prize in a show-jumping competition! The girl with the yellow mane showed me the paper this morning. "Of course, he is clever," she said. "But I would rather do dressage."

I just want to run in the forest. Rush around among the crackling leaves. Jump over stumps and chase along the paths. The forest is exciting. We haven't explored it that often. I become so wild there, everybody says. The trainer has taken me out a couple of times. And I've gone there myself with the little girls. That's fun. I run ahead, snorting, and they rush after, shouting. Back and forth we run.

I hope dressage means running in the forest!

DRESSAGE • Precision riding done at different degrees of difficulty, from programs with simple movements and different paces to difficult programs at Olympic level, which might include change of leg while cantering and piafe.

SHOW JUMPING • Competitions at different heights, with fences from twenty inches to over five feet high. The course can also have other difficulties, such as sharp turns. The fences vary in appearance and can be combined in many ways.

EVENTING • Includes both dressage and show jumping and also cross-country riding on a horse or a pony, at high speed, while jumping difficult fences. Here, too, there are competitions from beginner level to Olympic.

27

Fence

Electric wire

Electric tape

APRIL
12

Today I can stay out in the pasture all day for the first time this year. The girl with the yellow mane promised me yesterday. I woke up early and thought about my brother. I haven't seen him since I was ill. Perhaps he will be conceited, now that he has won a competition again. And what if he doesn't recognize me? I'm not fat anymore—just a little bit chubby.

Patch made me feel better. He was mewing about what fun it would be and about the tasty green grass, so I nearly knocked over the girl with the yellow mane when she came to fetch me at last.

28

BARBED WIRE
Can give the horse bad tear wounds.

SHEEP NETTING
The horse's hoof can get stuck in the fence and hurt.

When she shut the gate behind me and I had sniffed the air with my nostrils for a while, my legs went all frisky with happiness. I set off down the slope. Made a sharp turn, gamboled, and trotted up again. And so I carried on for a long while until I remembered about the salt lick. The taste made me remember summer. I licked my muzzle. Then the gate flew open, and in rushed two ponies at a wild gallop. We rushed up toward the next pasture, all three of us, and were in such a spring frenzy that the fence between us and my brother fell over. The electric wire sparked, and suddenly we realized we were all in the same pasture. We were together again, and summer is on its way!

FACT REGISTER